Daisy May + Angel

D1647220

Fashion Fairy
Princess

BR100

Bristol Libraries

1805408405

Thanks fairy much Sally Morgan!

First published in the UK in 2014 by Scholastic Children's Books
An imprint of Scholastic Ltd
Euston House, 24 Eversholt Street
London, NW1 1DB, UK
Registered office: Westfield Road, Southam, Warwickshire, CV47 0RA
SCHOLASTIC and associated logos are trademarks and/or registered
trademarks of Scholastic Inc.

Text copyright © Scholastic Ltd, 2014
Cover copyright © Pixie Potts, Beehive Illustration Agency, 2014
Inside illustration copyright © David Shephard, The Bright Agency, 2014

The right of Poppy Collins to be identified as the author
of this work has been asserted by her.

ISBN 978 1407 14590 7

A CIP catalogue record for this book is available from the British Library.

All rights reserved.
This book is sold subject to the condition that it shall not, by way of trade or
otherwise, be lent, hired out or otherwise circulated in any form of binding
or cover other than that in which it is published. No part of this publication
may be reproduced, stored in a retrieval system, or transmitted in any form or
by any means (electronic, mechanical, photocopying, recording or otherwise)
without the prior written permission of Scholastic Limited.

Printed and bound by CPI Group (UK) Ltd, Croydon, CR0 4YY
Papers used by Scholastic Children's Books are made
from wood grown in sustainable forests.

1 3 5 7 9 10 8 6 4 2

This is a work of fiction. Names, characters, places,
incidents and dialogues are products of the author's imagination
or are used fictitiously. Any resemblance to actual people, living
or dead, events or locales is entirely coincidental.

www.scholastic.co.uk
www.fashionfairyprincess.com

Angel catten

Fashion Fairy Princess

Primrose
in Jewel Forest

POPPY COLLINS

SCHOLASTIC

Dream
Mountain

Jewel Forest

Sparkle
City

Star
Valley

River
Sapphire

Shimmer Island

Glitter Ocean

Welcome to the world of the
fashion fairy princesses! Join Primrose
and friends on their magical adventures
in fairyland.

They can't wait to explore

Jewel Forest!

Can you?

Chapter 1

"Oh, Primrose! Your room looks beautiful," said Fluff Tail as she hopped into Princess Primrose's bedroom. "Thank you so much for inviting me to stay!"

"Not at all, Fluff Tail," said Primrose, putting her arm around the excited bunny rabbit. "Thank *you* for coming! Nutmeg and I just love sleepovers. We are going to have so much fun."

Fluff Tail hadn't been to a sleepover at the Tree Palace before and she was very excited. The palace was built into an ancient diamond-nut tree in the heart of the magical Jewel Forest. It was where the king and queen of the forest fairies lived with their two beautiful daughters, Princess Primrose and Nutmeg. Fluff Tail had been to parties in the trunk of the Tree Palace but had never been up into the branches, where the royal bedrooms could be found.

Primrose's bedroom was in a branch close to the top of the tree. It had beautiful polished wooden walls and lots of large leaf-shaped windows that looked out on to Jewel Forest. Fluff Tail hopped over to one of the windows and peered out on to the glittering trees below.

"My goodness!" said Fluff Tail. "I've never seen the forest from this high up. I think I might even be able to see my lovely little house if the clouds weren't quite so low."

"Not quite," said Primrose, laughing and tucking her glossy nut-brown plait neatly between her glittering yellow wings, "but you can certainly see a long way."

"What was that?" said Fluff Tail, looking hard into the darkening forest. "And another one. . . I think I just saw a raindrop. They look very different from up here, don't they? It must be starting to rain."

"Oh, I do hope so!" said Primrose, fluttering to her bunny friend's side. "I love to look out of the window when it rains, especially at night when the moonlight glints through the raindrops and makes them glow like milky-white gemstones."

"That sounds beautiful," said Fluff Tail, smiling.

"It is," said Primrose excitedly, "and it's even better when the wind blows, too! It rushes through the branches and around the trunk, making a beautiful whistling sound, like lots of forest fairy flutes playing all at once. It's magical and—"

Primrose stopped as her bedroom door swung open and an enormous tray, piled high with delicious sleepover treats, entered the room. Fluttering behind, and almost hidden by the huge tray she was carrying, was a small fairy with choppy

nut-brown hair and glittering orange
wings, who was wearing leaf-patterned
pyjamas with fluffy slippers.
It was Primrose's little sister,
Nutmeg.

"Hello, Fluff
Tail! I'm so
glad you
came," said
Nutmeg,
placing the

rose-coloured wooden tray on Primrose's
bed. "I asked the palace kitchen to make
your favourite carrot cupcakes."

"I hope you didn't go to any trouble,
Nutmeg," said Fluff Tail, hopping over to
the bed and eyeing the tray of yummy-
looking cakes hungrily.

"No trouble at all!" said Nutmeg,
smiling and popping one of the orange-

frosted cakes into her mouth. "Primrose and I love them, too."

"Ooh, is that a bottle of forest fizz?" asked Primrose, pointing at a glittery glass bottle. "I do hope it's ruby-currant flavour."

"It is!" said Nutmeg, handing her a cup.

"My favourite!" said Primrose. "Fluff Tail, have you tried it before?"

"It's delicious!" said Fluff Tail, giggling and twitching her little pink nose. "And I love the way the bubbles make my nose tickle."

When they had finished the delicious tray of goodies, the full-up fairies flopped back on to Primrose's bed, and Fluff Tail let out a groan, looking at the empty plates.

"I'm so full," she said, rubbing her round tummy with her soft silvery paws.

"Me, too!" said Primrose, laughing. "I

suppose we won't be needing a midnight feast after all."

"Mmm, no. . ." said Nutmeg, smiling sleepily.

"Good thing, too," said Fluff Tail. "My cousins Eloise and Silver are coming to stay with me at my burrow tomorrow, and I want to be home early to get everything ready for them."

Fluff Tail lived in a burrow called

Sapphire Lodge. It was dug into the roots of a beautiful sapphire tree a short walk from the Tree Palace.

"Listen to the rain now," said Primrose. "It sounds like there might be a storm. We'd better close the shutters on the windows before we go to sleep."

"I hope it's a storm," said Nutmeg. "There's nothing nicer than being all tucked up and cosy, listening to the wind howling outside. It's so exciting."

"Don't you get a bit scared, being this high up when the wind is blowing so hard?" asked Fluff Tail.

"Not at all," said Nutmeg. "This tree has been here for ever! It'll take more than a little storm to blow it— Eeeeek! What was that?"

Nutmeg wrapped her slim freckled arms around the bunny's soft body, startled by

 a sudden crashing sound outside. "Nutmeg!" said Primrose, laughing gently at her funny little sister. "That was just a bit of thunder."

"I know *that*," said Nutmeg, blushing, a little embarrassed for having made such a fuss.

Primrose walked over and held her sister's hand. "Perhaps you'd better sleep in here with us tonight," she said gently.

"Oh yes! Please can I?" said Nutmeg, cheering up instantly. "Not because I'm scared, of course, but I do hate missing out on all the fun. I'll go and get the hammocks!"

Nutmeg fluttered through a little wooden door and into her room, which was right next door to her sister's and just as beautiful.

"Hammocks?" said Fluff Tail. "How exciting! I've never slept in a hammock before. I usually sleep on my little pine bed."

"You're going to love sleeping in a hammock," said Primrose. "They're made of leaves and jewel-moth silk and are *so* comfortable."

As she spoke, Nutmeg fluttered back into the room carrying two hammocks, and the fairies hung them up on either side of Primrose's four-poster bed.

"What do you think, Fluff Tail?"

"They do look very comfortable," agreed Fluff Tail, "but how will I get in? I can't fly like you and Nutmeg."

"Easy," said Nutmeg. "You just jump

up on to the bed and then hop in."
Nutmeg demonstrated, gracefully fluttering
up on to the bed and bouncing into her
soft hammock.

"OK," said Fluff Tail, a little doubtfully.
She took a big hop up on to Primrose's bed
and then a small hop into the hammock
on the other side and was instantly
wrapped up in the soft jewel-moth silk.

"Oh my," said the sleepy bunny. "I don't think I have ever felt anything so comfortable."

"Aren't they wonderful?" said Nutmeg.

"I'm almost jealous," said Primrose, laughing as she climbed into her bed between the two hammocks.

As the two fairies and the sleepy rabbit settled down to sleep, they could hear the wind whistling its beautiful music through the branches of the tree palace.

"It sounds like quite a storm out there," said Nutmeg, snuggling deeper into her soft hammock.

"What's that chiming sound?" said Fluff Tail.

"It's the diamond nuts," said Primrose. "They chime like that when big raindrops fall on them."

"It's so beautiful, I don't want to fall

asleep," said Fluff Tail. "I want to stay awake and listen to it."

"Me, too," said Nutmeg. "Let's try and stay awake as long as we can."

"OK," said Primrose, "but I hope there isn't any more thunder. We don't want you falling out of your hammock, eh, Nutmeg?"

The three friends laughed and tried their hardest to stay awake, listening to the storm outside, but the magical music

it was making was starting to act like a soothing lullaby, and very soon they all fell fast asleep.

Chapter 2

"What was that?" cried Fluff Tail the next morning, forgetting for a moment that she wasn't in her own bed and almost falling out of her soft hammock. "I thought I heard a—"

Cuckoo!

"A cuckoo! I did, I heard a cuckoo!" cried the startled bunny.

Cuckoo! *Cuckoo*!

"Wake up! Primrose! Nutmeg!" Fluff Tail hopped down from the hammock and started looking around Primrose's room. "There must be a cuckoo trapped in the Tree Palace somewhere."

Cuckoo! *Cuckoo*! *Cuckoo*!

"It's OK, Fluff Tail," said Primrose, sitting up in her four-poster bed and smiling at her furry friend. "It's just my cuckoo clock. It does that every morning when it's time to for me to get up. Look!"

Primrose pointed towards a pink house-shaped clock hanging on the carved wall next to her bed. As she pointed, a tiny wooden cuckoo flew out of the house, shouted *Cuckoo*! and then fluttered over to land on Princess Primrose's extended finger.

"See, Fluff Tail?" said Primrose, holding the cuckoo for Fluff Tail to get a closer look. "It isn't a real cuckoo but a magical wooden one that lives in the clock."

The tiny cuckoo hopped off Primrose's delicate finger and on to the puzzled rabbit's twitching pink nose.

"Oh yes!" said Fluff Tail, laughing. "I can see that now. The Tree Palace really is amazing!"

"If you think *that's* amazing," said Nutmeg, sitting up in her hammock and giving a big yawn, "just wait until you see breakfast."

Princess Primrose and Nutmeg put on their satin dressing gowns and fluffy slippers and walked over to a carved panel in Primrose's bedroom wall. Primrose felt the wall for a small ear-shaped knot in the wood and whispered gently into it. "Please take us to the breakfast room," she breathed in a voice so quiet Fluff Tail could barely hear her.

As soon as she spoke, the wooden panel slid to one side and the sisters walked through it and down a winding, narrow staircase, with Fluff Tail hopping behind.

Fluff Tail chuckled. The Tree Palace was so different from her simple, comfortable home.

As Fluff Tail hopped out of the narrow passage and into the Tree Palace's breakfast room, she gasped. In front of her stood a beautifully laid buffet table that was covered with a glittering white

tablecloth sprinkled with tiny jewel nuts.
On top of the glittering cloth, pink
wooden platters held a mountain of delicious
treats. There were warm jewel-nut rolls,
ruby strawberries dipped in forest-honey
cream, and even more carrot cupcakes.

"Help yourself, Fluff Tail," said Primrose,
handing the hungry bunny a plate.

Primrose, Nutmeg and Fluff Tail each filled a plate with breakfast treats and took a crystal goblet of forest-fruit juice. The three friends sat at a table in front of the large stained-glass window at the end of the carved wooden breakfast room.

"That was quite a storm last night," said Primrose, taking a bite from a delicious-looking emerald-berry pancake. "I hope it didn't keep you awake, Fluff Tail."

"Not at all," said Fluff Tail, scooping the carrot frosting off one of the cupcakes and popping it into her mouth with her fluffy paw. "I slept very well. But I am looking forward to getting home and seeing my cousins."

"Eloise and Silver?" asked Primrose.

"Yes!" said Fluff Tail. "It's been so long since I last saw them. I've been

tidying up my little garden and getting
things ready for them all week. I just
hope the storm didn't make too much of
a mess."

"We'll help you tidy it, if it has," said
Primrose, reassuring her friend. "Nutmeg
and I will walk you back after breakfast."

"Oh yes!" said Nutmeg excitedly, almost
spilling her juice. "We love to walk
through the forest after a storm. The rain
knocks some of the loveliest nuts from the
tops of the tree branches. Primrose, can
we take our baskets to collect them?"

"Of course, Nutmeg," said Primrose, laughing at her enthusiastic little sister.

"Let's flutter upstairs and get dressed. Fluff Tail, we'll meet you back here in two ticks of a dandelion clock." And with that the two fairies zoomed out of the breakfast room.

Fluff Tail barely had time to take another sip of her delicious juice before Primrose and Nutmeg fluttered back in, wearing emerald-green raincoats and sparkly jade green wellies. Nutmeg was carrying an enormous glittery basket and Primrose was holding a lilac satin umbrella with a golden handle.

"Hi, Fluff Tail," said Primrose. "Are you ready to go? I know you didn't bring your raincoat, so I thought you could use this," she said, holding out the umbrella.

"That's so thoughtful of you,

Primrose," said Fluff Tail. She took the umbrella and then followed her fairy friends down a huge sweeping staircase all the way to the bottom of the Tree Palace and then out into the forest.

Jewel Forest looked more shimmering and magical than ever. The glittering raindrops clung to the leaves and branches and made them super-sparkly in the dappled morning sunlight. Nutmeg fluttered ahead, collecting jewel nuts, while Primrose and Fluff Tail walked along behind.

"Don't you just love the smell of Jewel Forest after the rain?" said Primrose, grinning. "I'm so glad I said we would walk you back, Fluff Tail. What time do your cousins arrive?"

"At teatime," said Fluff Tail. "I've ordered fancy cakes from Blossom's Bakery just for them."

"Mmm, delicious. Blossom's moonbutter cupcakes are the best!" said Nutmeg, licking her lips as she plucked a glittering nut from a fallen branch before zooming off to find another.

As they continued up the path, Fluff Tail had to slow down – there were lots of fallen branches and even some uprooted trees that she had to hop over and scrabble through. "My garden is going to be more of a mess than I thought," said Fluff Tail, scrambling over a glittering tree branch. "It looks like the storm winds blew a lot harder here."

"Don't worry, Nutmeg and I will help clear it up," said Primrose. "And we can always get Catkin to help. She's wonderful with plants. Oh look, I think I see some candy-tufted tree squirrels up ahead."

"Hello, Conker and Sycamore," said Primrose, greeting the fluffy pink squirrels with a friendly hug. "We heard the big storm last night. How are all the squirrels?"

"We're fine," said Conker, "but a few houses weren't so lucky."

"Oh dear, I do hope my house is all right," said Fluff Tail, peering nervously up the path.

"I'm sure it will be," said Primrose, putting her arm around her friend. "Let's go and see it now."

"Sycamore and I will come with you," said Conker.

As she hopped up the path, Fluff Tail began to worry. *So many trees have been blown down. Please let my little house still be there*, she thought to herself, but as they got closer her heart fell.

"Oh no!" Fluff Tail cried. "My beautiful home!" Primrose crouched down to give her friend a hug. The rabbit buried her furry face in Primrose's shoulder, not wanting to look at the fallen sapphire tree in front of her. The tree was lying on its side with its

roots – usually buried deep into the
soil – reaching up into the air. Tangled
among the roots and scattered around the
forest floor were all Fluff Tail's precious
belongings.

Chapter 3

"Oh, Fluff Tail!" said Primrose, stroking her friend's soft ears. "I'm so, so, sorry."

"Here," said Nutmeg, tipping all the glittering nuts out of her

basket. "I'll collect what I can in my basket."

Nutmeg bent down and carefully picked up one of Fluff Tail's broken wooden chairs from the mess.

"Thank you, Nutmeg," said Fluff Tail, sobbing. "It's so kind of you to help, but I won't have anywhere to put any of the things you save. My lovely home is ruined and I have nowhere to go."

"You can come and stay with me," said Conker. "We squirrels love having company."

"That's a great idea," said Primrose. "You can stay with Conker until we find you a new house."

"But I don't want a new home," said Fluff Tail sadly, nudging some of the wilted carrot plants in her once-perfect garden. "I loved this one. And I was

so excited about showing it to Eloise
and Silver too. They'll be on their way
shortly – how can I tell them not to
come?"

"Don't worry about your cousins. I'll go
to the post office right away and send them
an urgent fairy-mail telling them what has
happened," said Primrose gently. "I promise
that we'll find you a wonderful home, Fluff
Tail. Even more beautiful and comfortable
than Sapphire Lodge."

"And until we find one," Conker
added, "you'll have a jolly time staying
with us squirrels. Come with me and
I'll make you a delicious cup of calming
diamond–nut tea."

Fluff Tail nodded sadly, thanked her
fairy friends and hopped away with the
scampering squirrels.

"Poor Fluff Tail," said Nutmeg,

gathering up some of Fluff Tail's carved wooden spoons and forks and putting them in her sparkly basket.

"I know," said Primrose thoughtfully, "and she was so excited about her cousins coming to stay. There must be something more we can do. I'll have a think on my way to the post office. Will you be OK here on your own, Nutmeg?"

"Of course," said Nutmeg, popping a pretty teapot into her basket, "and Sycamore and the squirrels said they'll be back to help."

"Excellent," said Primrose, "the more

paws the better. We're going to need as much help as we can get."

With that the thoughtful princess fluttered high up into the trees and along the forest fairy skyway to the post office. The skyway was a delicate network of glittering leafy bridges that connected all the houses and shops in Jewel Forest.

As she flew, Primrose was thinking so much about Fluff Tail that she didn't notice her good friend Catkin up ahead on the skyway.

"Hello, Primrose!" called Catkin, pushing a strand of curly red hair out of her face and fluttering her red-tipped wings after her distracted friend. "Where are you off to in such a hurry?"

"Oh, hi, Catkin," said Primrose. "I'm sorry, I didn't see you. I'm just so worried about Fluff Tail."

"Fluff Tail?" said Catkin, puzzled. "Why, what's happened?"

"Her house was blown down in the storm," said Primrose. "It's so sad. I was just on my way to the post office to send an urgent fairy-mail to her cousins from Dream Mountain. They were supposed to be coming to visit her today. It seems such a shame to cancel their trip, but she has nowhere for them to stay."

"Poor Fluff Tail," said Catkin. "That's awful. I'm just on my way to meet Willa at the Dewdrop Diamond Inn. Why don't you come with me and we can put our heads together and see what we can do to help?"

"I'd love to come with you," said Primrose, "but I really should get going. Wait – the Dewdrop Diamond, you say. . . Of course! Catkin, you are a genius! Perhaps the Dewdrop will have rooms for Fluff Tail's cousins!"

"It's definitely worth a try," said Catkin. "Let's hurry there now and see!"

Primrose and Catkin fluttered towards the inn as fast as their glittering wings would carry them.

Chapter 4

The Dewdrop Diamond Inn had been carved into the trunk of a purple-jewelled tree by a family of woodpeckers a very long time ago. It was still run by the same woodpeckers' great-great-great-grandchildren. Fairies and magical creatures from all over fairyland stayed there when they came to visit their forest fairy friends.

As Primrose and Catkin approached the carved wooden door of the inn, they spotted a pair of glittering pink wings up ahead of them on the skyway.

"Willa!" Primrose cried, fluttering her wings as fast as she could to catch up with her fairy friend. "Hello there! Wait for us!"

"Hello, Primrose," said Willa. "My goodness, you are in a hurry! Whatever in fairyland is the matter?"

"Oh, Willa," said Primrose, giving her friend a breathless hug. "It's Fluff Tail.

Nutmeg and I walked her home through the forest this morning only, to find that her little house was destroyed in last night's storm."

"That's dreadful!" said Willa. "Come inside for a forest-nut chocolate and we'll come up with a plan to help."

The three friends walked into the sunny inn and settled down next to a large window that looked out on to the magical forest. As they waited for one of the woodpeckers to come and take their order, Primrose told her friends how pleased she was to have bumped into them.

"You're so good at organizing things, Catkin, and Willa, you always know what to do in a crisis. I just know that if we three put our heads together, we'll find a home for Fluff Tail in no time."

"Well, we will with you in charge, Primrose," said Willa, taking off her ivy-leaf rain hat and shaking out her long dark hair. "You are so good and kind to all the magical creatures in Jewel Forest that I'm sure that everyone will want to return the sweet little favours you've done for them."

Just then, a smartly dressed woodpecker with spectacles perched on his beak hopped over to the table.

"Hello there, Princess Primrose, how are you today? Can I get you and your friends your usual?" he asked, smiling.

"Hello, Glitter Beak," said Primrose. "Yes, three forest-nut chocolates with extra foam, please. Also, do you by any chance have a room available tonight for two rabbits?"

"You know," said Glitter Beak, with a

wink, "I think we do. I just received a
fairy-mail from a family of voles saying
they couldn't make their trip because of
the storm. The room would be perfect
for two bunny rabbits."

"Oh, that's wonderful news," said
Primrose, clapping her hands. "Please could
you prepare our forest-nut chocolates so we
can take them with us? We need to send a
fairy-mail to let Eloise and Silver know."

"Eloise and Silver," said Glitter Beak, "they're Fluff Tail's cousins, aren't they? Why can't they stay with Fluff Tail?"

Primrose took a deep breath, and with a heavy heart she told Glitter Beak all about Fluff Tail's home and the storm.

"Say no more," said Glitter Beak. "Please let Fluff Tail know that her cousins will be welcome to stay as long as they like. Free of charge. Also, if there is any building work you need doing, we woodpeckers would be honoured to help. We can make furniture, too!"

"Oh, Glitter Beak," said Primrose, hugging the black-and-white woodpecker, "that's so kind of you! You woodpeckers are the best builders in Jewel Forest!"

Glitter Beak flushed under his feathers at the compliment, and hopped off to fetch the fairies' drinks.

"Right," said Catkin, "that's Eloise and Silver taken care of, and any building and furniture we need doing. What next?"

"Well," said Primrose, thinking hard, "furniture isn't going to be much use without a lovely little house to put it in. Let's head into the forest to see if we can find Fluff Tail a home."

"Good idea," said Willa. "The more of us looking the quicker we will find the perfect spot."

Glitter Beak returned with three cups made from cleverly folded leaves and handed one to each of the fairies.

"Good luck!" he said. "And please let me know if there's anything more us woodpeckers can do to help. Fluff Tail is a dear friend."

"We will," said Primrose, "and thank you so much."

And with that the three fairy friends whooshed out of the door so fast they almost knocked the foam off their forest-nut chocolates.

Chapter 5

Princess Primrose, Catkin and Willa
headed to the post office to send the
fairy-mail to Eloise and Silver, sipping
their drinks as they went.

"Mmm," said Willa, taking a sip
from the leaf cup, "the Dewdrop
makes the best forest-nut chocolate.
I'm really enjoying mine."

Catkin giggled "We can tell," she said,
wiping a little blob of foam off Willa's

nose with the tip of her delicate finger.

The three friends laughed and Primrose's heart felt a little lighter, until she caught sight of the long queue stretching from the forest fairy post office ahead of them.

In the queue stood forest fairies wearing sparkly outfits made from leaves and glittering cobwebs, candy-tufted tree squirrels with shimmering pink fur, and little birds and insects.

Everyone in the queue was holding a letter or a leaf-wrapped parcel ready to send by fairy-mail to someone far away in fairyland.

Primrose's heart sank as she took her place in the queue. *This is going to take for ever*, she thought to herself, *and we still have so much to do!*

"Whatever is the matter, Princess Primrose?" asked a pretty robin standing just ahead of Primrose, who had noticed the princess's sad face. All the robin's feathers were brown except for a shining apron of bright ruby feathers on his round tummy. It was Primrose's good friend, Little Hop.

"Oh, Little Hop!" said Primrose, recognizing her ruby-red-breasted friend. "It's Fluff Tail." The friendly robin placed his package on the skyway in front of him and listened with his feathered head cocked to one side as Primrose told him all about Fluff Tail losing her home in the storm.

"And now we need to send an urgent fairy-mail to Fluff Tail's cousins," Primrose continued, waving her delicate hand towards the long queue snaking along the skyway, "but I don't see us reaching the front of this queue before nightfall."

"We'll see about that," said the robin. Little Hop thought for a moment, and then his feathered face lit up. His glittering black eyes twinkled with excitement as he hopped up on to the handrail of the skyway and then addressed the chattering post office queue ahead of him.

"Hello there, everyone," cheeped the little robin. The crowd of fairies and forest creatures fell silent and turned to look at him. "I was wondering if you

could do me – or rather my friend
Princess Primrose – a small favour."
Little Hop waved one of his little
brown wings towards Primrose and the
queue all looked in the direction he was
pointing.

Now it was time for Primrose to
speak, and although she was nervous, she
knew she had to be very brave to help

her friend Fluff Tail.

Primrose cleared her throat with a delicate cough and then spoke in a clear tone that everyone could hear.

"Hello, everyone," she said with a smile, "I would like your attention because I really need your help. You see, our friend Fluff Tail the rabbit is in a terrible mess. I'm sure you all heard the storm last night?"

Everyone in the queue nodded.

"Well, the storm was so big that it took down some of the trees in our beloved forest. Among those was the sapphire tree that held Fluff Tail's lovely little house among its roots."

The queue gasped in shock.

"Is . . . is Fluff Tail OK?" asked a shimmering jewel moth who was holding a bright purple envelope.

"Yes," said Primrose. "Thankfully she was staying with Nutmeg and me for a sleepover. But she has lost everything, including her beautiful garden. My friends and I are looking for a new home for Fluff Tail and we would be so grateful if you could let us know if you can think of anywhere."

The queue erupted in chatter as the fairies and forest creatures all shared ideas of places they thought might be suitable.

"Oh! Wait a minute," shouted Catkin above the chattering queue. "We need one more favour. Please could you let us to the front of the queue so that we can send an urgent fairy-mail?"

As she spoke, the queue moved to one side, everyone smiling kindly, and the fairy friends zoomed straight to the

front and into the post office to send
their urgent message to Eloise and Silver.

Chapter 6

With the urgent fairy-mail on its way, the three friends pushed open the door of the post office with a little tinkle and fluttered into a sea of smiling faces outside.

Standing at the front was Little Hop. "We think we've found the perfect place for Fluff Tail. . ." the little robin said excitedly. "In a ruby tree. One of the tree squirrels says it's not far from here and that its roots would be perfect for a rabbit's burrow."

"Well, what are we waiting for?" said Primrose, clapping her hands. "Let's go and take a look."

And with that Little Hop led the friends further into Jewel Forest to go in search of the ruby tree.

Primrose now felt rather excited as she skipped and fluttered along the skyway with Willa and Catkin. They chatted together about how happy Fluff Tail would be in the new home they were going to find for her. They were so busy talking, in fact, that they didn't notice that something very odd was going on. It wasn't until they had passed Bluebell Clearing, crossed Crystal Creek and were just approaching the enormous tree with its glittering red trunk that Primrose heard some chattering just behind her. She turned round to see that everyone in the queue for the post office had followed them, all clutching the letters and parcels they'd wanted to send.

Primrose smiled at the crowd, but was a little confused about why they had followed them. She was just about to ask when a smartly dressed forest fairy in a green suit and glossy holly-leaf hat stepped forward.

"I do hope you don't mind," said the

fairy, tucking a large parcel under her arm. "It's just that we all wanted to help, so we thought we would come along and see what needed doing."

"Of course," said Primrose, feeling so happy she could almost cry. She was so touched that everyone wanted to help her friend Fluff Tail. Jewel Forest really was a very special place to live. "Well, let's all take a closer look, shall we?" she said to the eager crowd.

As Primrose got closer to the tree, she could see that the squirrels were right. This really was the perfect place to build a new home for Fluff Tail.

The tree had thick roots around its trunk, one of which rose up in a neat arch just big enough for a rabbit to hop through. The ground around it was covered in glittering pine needles, but Primrose could tell that underneath there would be lots of nice soil for Fluff Tail to plant a lovely new garden.

"This is it!" said Primrose, grinning from ear to ear. "This will be Fluff Tail's new home, and with all Jewel Forest's help, I just know she'll be able to move in no time."

"Hooray!" everybody cheered, and
Primrose immediately set to work giving
the crowd of forest fairies and creatures
a job to do. Little Hop was sent to go
and fetch Nutmeg and some of the tree
squirrels.

"But make sure you tell them to keep
it a secret from Fluff Tail," said Primrose

with a little wink. "It'll be so much more fun if it's a surprise."

"Of course, princess," said Little Hop, giving a funny salute with his wing.

Willa fluttered back to the Dewdrop Diamond Inn to fetch the woodpeckers, while Catkin got to work clearing the ground around the trunk of the enormous ruby tree.

Primrose was just moving a large ruby cone from what would be the front door when she felt the soft flutter of silky wings as a jewel moth landed at her side.

"Hello, Princess Primrose, my name is Moonbeam," said the jewel moth in a voice as soft as her velvety purple wings. "I was just wondering if there was anything we jewel moths could do. We aren't very good at building or clearing, but we would so like to be able to help make this a home for Fluff Tail."

Primrose thought for a moment. Moonbeam was right. Moths weren't very good at building or clearing, and they couldn't even collect twigs to make furniture like the Jewel Forest birds. Primrose thought of Fluff Tail and what her home might need that only a jewel moth could give. It was then that an idea came to her, and the fairy princess leant forward and whispered to the waiting jewel moth.

When Moonbeam heard what Primrose wanted, she smiled and immediately flew off into the forest.

Chapter 7

With so many of Fluff Tail and Primrose's friends helping, work on the new house went very quickly and was even good fun! Catkin and the forest fairies cleared all the glittering pine needles from around the ruby tree's roots and had just started turning the soil for the brand-new garden when Willa returned with the woodpeckers. They put their strong beaks to work, hollowing out the doorway with a very loud *tap, tap, tap*.

Glitter Beak arrived soon after with a basket filled with scrummy sandwiches and flasks of hot forest-nut chocolate for all the workers to enjoy.

Not long after, Little Hop and the other Jewel Forest birds came back to the ruby tree with their beaks filled with twigs and helped Glitter Beak build a little table and bed for Fluff Tail.

Primrose stood for a moment to admire all the hard work that was going on around her. At that moment she spotted Nutmeg zooming along the skyway, followed by the candy-tufted tree squirrels. They were carrying armfuls of items they had managed to rescue from Sapphire Lodge.

"Nutmeg!" called Primrose loudly over the *tap, tap, tap* of the woodpeckers. "Down here!"

Nutmeg smiled and flew down from the skyway, dropping her basket and wrapping her freckled arms around her sister in a huge hug.

"Oh, Primrose," said Nutmeg, flapping her glittering orange wings excitedly. "I can't believe how much you've done already! I just know Fluff Tail is going to love it. And look, did you see how many of her things we managed to save! Conker even managed to rescue some of Fluff Tail's precious plants from her garden!"

"Oh, that's wonderful," said Primrose. "Catkin can plant them right away."

Primrose was about to continue when she realized she was shouting and that the loud *tap, tap, tap* of the woodpeckers' beaks had stopped.

"Oh, my fairyness," said Primrose, running over to what was now a beautiful doorway at the foot of the tall ruby tree. "Have you finished?"

"Far from it," said Glitter Beak, looking worried. "We're going to need some diggers."

"Diggers?" said Primrose, looking a bit confused. "What for? Can't you just burrow into the trunk with your beaks?"

"Well, we could," said Glitter Beak. "We could do that very easily. The only thing is that rabbits like Fluff Tail live

underground, not inside trees, and our beaks won't burrow into the soil."

"Oh no!" said Primrose, cross with herself. "Why didn't I think of that? We don't have anyone to dig. Fairies are hopeless diggers, with our tiny hands and our wings getting in the way, and even though the squirrels can dig a little, they can't tunnel like rabbits. Whatever will we do now? I hate to think that everyone's hard work has been for nothing."

Primrose gazed around at all her Jewel Forest friends working side by side and knew that she was about to cry. Just as the first tear rolled down her soft cheek, she felt a feathered wing against her shoulder. It was Little Hop.

"Why are you so sad, Princess Primrose?" said the little robin, nuzzling her with his soft downy head. "Look around you! Look at how much you've managed to do for Fluff Tail. You've organized everyone and got them to work miracles! Thanks to you, Fluff Tail will have a new home by tonight."

"No, she won't," said Primrose sadly. "And it's all my fault. I completely forgot that rabbits live underground and we don't have any diggers! We've made beautiful furniture and a gorgeous garden. We even have a beautiful doorway, but it doesn't lead anywhere."

Little Hop thought for a moment and then laughed to himself. "Well, if that's all you're worried about," said the robin cheekily, "it's an easy problem to fix."

"But how, Little Hop? I don't understand what you mean," said Primrose.

"Well," said the robin, hopping up and down with excitement, "there just happen to be two diggers sitting on their fluffy tails at the Dewdrop Diamond Inn thanks to you."

"Of course!" said Primrose, giving him a kiss on the beak. "Eloise and Silver. Who better to dig a home fit for a bunny rabbit. I'll go and get them right away."

"No need," said Glitter Beak, smiling and pointing at two excited bunnies hopping towards them.

Chapter 8

"Eloise! Silver!" called Primrose to the two rabbits hopping quickly towards her. "You've no idea how glad I am to see you."

"Hello, Princess Primrose," said Silver, a small round rabbit with silvery soft fur. "We were so grateful to receive your message. Thank you. Our room at the inn is just lovely, but we couldn't sit and enjoy it while all this work was going on and our poor cousin Fluff Tail was without a home."

"Indeed," said Eloise, a well-spoken rabbit with darker, shinier fur than Silver. "How can we help?"

"You came at just the right time," said Primrose, smiling. She walked the two rabbits over to where the woodpeckers had just finished carving the entrance into the root of the ruby tree.

"Goodness me!" said Eloise, admiring the wooden doors. "This is beautiful. How many bedrooms does it have?"

"Well, that's up to you," said Primrose nervously, as she explained how

desperately they needed someone to dig
the rest of the home.

Eloise and Silver looked at each other
for a moment and then smiled.

"It would be our pleasure, Primrose.
Eloise is the best digger I know," said
Silver, patting Eloise on her soft back.

"I'm not sure that I am the best
digger," said Eloise shyly, "but I will
certainly try my hardest."

"Oh, thank you! Thank you!" said
Princess Primrose.

Eloise and Silver started at once,
digging into the rich soil, while the
forest fairies worked together, putting
the finishing touches to Fluff Tail's new
home.

The birds and woodpeckers had made
a beautiful bed from rosewood that was
just the right height for the little bunny

to hop on to easily. They'd also built
a table, four comfortable chairs and a
gorgeous set of mugs made from acorn cups.

Primrose's sister, Nutmeg, gathered all
the things she and the tree squirrels had
rescued, and worked with Willa and Little
Hop to repair what they could, including
a shiny, silver-framed photograph of
Princess Primrose with her arm around
Fluff Tail.

The items were carefully laid out on

Fluff Tail's brand-new table outside the beautifully carved entrance.

"Just look at these lovely things," said Primrose to Nutmeg. "I do hope Fluff Tail will be happy here. I hated seeing her so sad this morning."

"Primrose! Nutmeg! I'm really sorry!" a voice called from behind them.

The fairy princess sisters spun round to see Conker the candy-tufted tree squirrel running towards them.

"Conker, whatever is the matter?" said Primrose to the breathless squirrel. "Is something wrong with Fluff Tail?"

"Not wrong, no," gasped Conker. "It's just that she's on her way here. She wanted to go for a walk and got suspicious when I tried to stop her. I ran as fast as I could, but she won't be far behind me. I really am sorry."

"Oh, Conker," Primrose laughed, "don't be sorry. Everything is very nearly ready!"

She turned to the group of busy creatures. "Action stations, everyone!" she called. "Fluff Tail is on her way! Let's see if we can get everything done before she arrives."

"Finished!" shouted Silver, hopping out of the tree and scampering over to Primrose. "Didn't I tell you Eloise was the best digger?"

"Oh, that's wonderful," said Primrose, clapping her hands. "Just in time! Let's get everything inside, quick!"

Eloise and Silver dusted off their soft fur and joined the rest of the fairies and forest creatures as they worked together to move Fluff Tail's lovely things into her new home.

Primrose and Conker waited outside

the carved doorway keeping a lookout
for Fluff Tail, and it wasn't long until
they saw her floppy ears as she bounced
towards them.

"Primrose, is that you?" called Fluff
Tail, hopping closer. "What are you
doing out in the forest? Ah, there you
are, Conker! You scurried off so fast
I couldn't keep up with you. What a
beautiful ruby tree!"

"Hello, Fluff Tail," said Primrose,
grinning. "It is a beautiful tree, isn't it?
I'm so glad you like it."

"Like it? What do you mean?" asked
Fluff Tail, confused.

"Well. . ." said Primrose, signalling to
her friends to come out.

"Surprise!" everyone yelled as they
poured out of the beautiful entrance the
woodpeckers had carved into the ruby tree.

"W—what?" stuttered Fluff Tail. "I
don't understand. Why is everyone here?"

"We're all here for you, Fluff Tail,"
said Primrose, hugging her puzzled friend.
"Everyone is here to welcome you to
your new home. Welcome to Ruby
Lodge!"

It was then that Eloise and Silver

hopped out of the little house and over to their startled cousin.

"Fluff Tail!" cried Eloise, wrapping Fluff Tail in her dark silver-grey paws. "Just wait and see what we've done inside!"

"Princess Primrose," said Fluff Tail, smiling, "I thought I asked you to send a fairy-mail to tell my cousins not to come."

"Ah well. . ." said Primrose. "I know you did, but I just thought. . ."

All the fairies and forest creatures who were gathered outside laughed. It was just like Primrose to do everything she could to help a friend.

"Thank you!" said Fluff Tail, reaching out a paw to Primrose and giving her tiny hand a little squeeze. "Thank you, Primrose, for everything. It's *beautiful*."

And with that Primrose followed Fluff Tail and her two very excited cousins into Ruby Lodge.

It really was beautiful! Eloise and Silver had dug a nice long entranceway that split off into two large rooms. The room on the left was the kitchen, with the table and chairs the woodpeckers had made. The room to the right was Fluff Tail's bedroom, with its lovely new bed. Fluff Tail hopped over to the little table next to the bed and, with her fluffy paw, touched the shiny silver frame that was perched on top of it. It was the picture of her with Primrose.

"You even saved my pictures," said Fluff Tail, letting out a little sniff.

She looked around at all her precious things in her brand-new home and smiled. "I so loved Sapphire Lodge, but I know I'm going to love Ruby Lodge even more. Just knowing that you all

put so much care into building it makes it a very special place indeed."

"There's just one problem," said Silver, glancing around Fluff Tail's comfortable bedroom. "There's only one bed. It's a very beautiful bed, but it won't fit all three of us rabbits in it. I suppose we'll have to stay at the Dewdrop Diamond Inn after all."

"No need," said Primrose, beaming. "I have one more surprise for you, Fluff Tail!"

Primrose flew out of the burrow, and

returned with Moonbeam the jewel moth, who was carrying an enormous bundle of the most beautiful softly shimmering silk any of them had ever seen.

"Princess Primrose told me that there might be a couple of bunnies in need of some hammocks," said the moth, placing his gorgeous bundle on to Fluff Tail's bed.

"Wow!" said Fluff Tail. "These are really beautiful, Moonbeam. Primrose, however did you manage to organize everyone? I don't know how I'll ever be able to repay you all."

"No need to repay us, Fluff Tail," said Nutmeg, grinning. "Everyone was glad to help, but I'm sure we wouldn't mind a few moonbutter cakes from Blossom's."

"The cakes!" said Fluff Tail. "Oh no! I completely forgot that Blossom was going to deliver them. She won't be able to find me now."

"Hello!" called a fairy from just inside the doorway. "Hello, is anybody there? I'm not sure if this is the right address. Is this Fluff Tail's new house?"

"Blossom!" cried Fluff Tail. "How did you manage to find me?"

"Easy!" smiled Blossom. "When I saw

what happened at Sapphire Lodge, I called in at the post office. They told me that this was your new home and that everyone would be here."

Blossom placed the enormous pink box she was carrying on Fluff Tail's new kitchen table. "I hope you don't mind. . . I didn't think there would be enough, so I popped in a few extra cupcakes," she added with a wink.

"In that case," said Fluff Tail, hopping with excitement, "let's have a house-warming party! Everyone help yourself to a moonbutter cake and I'll make a few pots of tea. I can't wait to try out my new cups and plates."

It was a little crowded in Ruby Lodge that night, and everyone was very tired, but all the forest fairies and creatures agreed that it had been a lovely party and

that Ruby Lodge was a very special place
to live indeed.

If you enjoyed this

Fashion Fairy Princess

book then why not visit our
magical new website!

- Explore the enchanted world of
  the fashion fairy princesses
- Find out which fairy princess
  you are
- Download sparkly screensavers
- Make your own tiara
- Colour in your own picture frame
  and much more!

fashionfairyprincess.com

Fashion Fairy Princess

Blossom

in Jewel Forest

Turn the page for a sneak peek of the next
Fashion Fairy Princess adventure...

Chapter 1

Blossom was pulling the latest tray of diamond-glitter brownies out of the bakery oven when she heard the door open and a little voice call out.

"Hi, Blossom, are you there?"

Blossom popped up her head from behind the counter and saw Pip standing in the doorway, waving and smiling. Her tiny forest fairy friend wore a gorgeous fern grass dress with

matching dangly earrings. Blossom
looked down at herself. She had icing
sugar all over her tights, dandelion flour
covered her apron, and she was certain
she had cake mixture stuck in her
unruly blonde hair!

"Oh, hello, Pip. I'm sorry I look
such a mess! It's all been a bit crazy
getting ready for the Jewel Forest fête
tomorrow."

Everyone loved the annual fête. Fairies
came from all over fairyland to join
in the fun and games – and to sample
Blossom's famous cakes!

"I thought it might be, so I wanted to
pop in and see how you were doing,"
said Pip. "You mustn't work too hard,
you know."

"But the cake sale is the highlight of
the fête!" Blossom took a tray of unbaked

muffins from the counter and slid them into the steaming hot oven. She threw in some more fairy-dust to keep up the temperature. "All the cakes have to be perfect!"

Pip looked around the bakery. Every single surface was covered. There were open bags of flour and sugar, cake stands in beautiful pastel colours, biscuits cooling, fairy buns with their icing setting, and bowls of mixture waiting to be put into moulds. She wondered whether Blossom would get everything done in time, but she didn't want to ask and risk hurting her friend's feelings. Blossom was the best baker in the forest, after all.

"While the muffins are baking, let me show you some of my cake designs," Blossom suggested, fluttering around the

counter and heading towards the walnut
table where customers usually sat. Today
that would have been impossible, as
it was covered in cake boxes – some
already made, some still flat and waiting
to be put together.

Pip moved a pile of unmade cake
boxes from a chair and placed them
carefully on the floor while Blossom
grabbed a large daisy-paper scrapbook
from the window sill.

"I've been working on the recipe for
the moonbutter cakes for weeks," said
Blossom, pointing to a pencil drawing of
cupcakes with butter icing in the shape
of crescent moons.

"Oh, they look delicious!" Pip peered
at the scrapbook. Blossom's drawings
were so detailed she could almost taste
them!

Blossom turned a page. "And this is how I've designed the diamond-glitter brownies. When they're put on to their cake stand, they'll look like a sparkling tree trunk!"

"What a great idea – and perfect for a forest fête," agreed Pip.

"Thanks, Pip," said Blossom, grinning. "And let me show you what I'm planning for the highlight of my stall. . ." Blossom flicked through the pages with her dough-covered fingers. "Here it is – the double-layer sunshine cake!"

A huge two-layer cake had been drawn on the page, with shimmering rays bursting out of the top. "It will be iced with edible jewels straight from the Jewel Tree, which will shoot rays of sunshine from the cake as you eat it. It's going

to be very special — I hope so, anyway."
The Jewel Tree was the first tree ever to
grow in the forest and the source of all
the forest fairy magic. Blossom closed the
scrapbook and jumped up. "I must check
on the muffins!"

She whizzed behind the bakery
counter and opened the oven. Mouth-
watering smells flooded out — chocolatey-
sugar sweetness. Pip breathed in deeply.
"Mmmmm, yum!"

Get creative with the fashion fairy princesses in these magical sticker-activity books!